I0665094

Destiny

By Amina N.

Destiny
Amina N.

ISBN 978-0-692-64933-6

Acknowledgments

I dedicate this book to my dear daughter Raisha. Thank you for being my rock, my beta reader, my most opinionated critic.

To Karimah Grayson, thank you for giving me the push that I needed to move forward when I doubted that my work was worth finishing.

To Papatia Feauxzar, I cannot thank you enough for all the help you have provided me. Your constructive criticism was truly valuable. I pray for your continued success.

To my mother and siblings, I could not be where I am today without all of you. Special thanks to my sister Mame. I shall always be grateful for having you in my life. There is nothing that you wouldn't do for me, and I want you to know that

I will never take you for granted. I love you all.

To my late father, thirty years after your passing I still do not miss you any less. I cherish all the memories that you left me with. May Allah have Mercy on you and grant you entry into the highest levels of Paradise.

I would like to express gratitude to Hend Hegazi for the excellent editing and valuable feedback you provided, all in a timely manner.

To my book cover designer Kaltrina Ferizi for your creativity; thank you for an amazing job.

Although this book was inspired by true events, it is a work of fiction. Names, characters, businesses, places, events and incidents are either the products of my imagination or used in a fictitious manner. Any resemblance to actual persons, living or dead, or actual events is purely coincidental. Abuse exists in circles in society and can affect men or women, Muslim or non Muslim, rich or poor independent of the person's place of origin. It's usually a taboo subject which makes the victim feels ashamed to seek help. Not speaking about it will not make it disappear. It's not okay to stigmatize those who are victims, neither is it okay for the victim to blame themselves, ignore the signs, or feel like they have the power to eventually change the person who is afflicting the violence on them, be it verbal or physical. The only way to eradicate abuse is for everyone in society to be honest about it, make the victims feel comfortable to speak out without being judged, and help the perpetrators understand that they need professional help.

Please refer to the Glossary at the end of the book for a translation of the Arabic terms.

Chapter One

Destiny walked towards the clubhouse down the street. Suddenly, the city of North Miami where she had grown up seemed foreign to her. The shadow of the palm trees underneath the dim lighting appeared to be moving creatures. She looked around to find a place where she could feel safe. The streets which were not very crowded during daytime hours gave the impression that the neighborhood was uninhabited in these wee hours of the night. She couldn't think of a safe place to go at three a.m.; she was unsure whether or not the poolside would do, but there was nowhere else she could think of going.

She scrolled through the list of contacts on her mobile phone, stopped when she saw her mother's phone number, and stared at it for a while. He finger remained suspended above the green dial icon, yet, she couldn't bring herself to tap on it. Warm tears rolled down her chocolate colored cheeks. She slipped the phone back into her pocket and started walking again.

Amina N.

She slowly opened the clubhouse gate looking around to make sure that she was alone. A rustling noise in the bushes forced her to race back towards the street. Right after that, a small being jumped the fence. Cold sweat gushed from each one of her pores, her heart beat tripled in speed. She couldn't hold her weight up anymore on seeing that it was just a cat that she had taken by surprise. She sat on the sidewalk, put her hand over her face and held it there. She did not want to see or hear scary things any longer.

She had been out on the street for about an hour now. Minutes on the clock seemed like hours that night. She didn't even have time to grab her car key when she rushed out of the house, she could have at least spent the night in the vehicle. Going back in there was out of the question now. She didn't have any other choice but to wait for day break.

She took a deep breath, curled into the fetal position, hoping to forget where she was. May be it was all a nightmare. She was probably laying on her bed in a deep sleep. All will go back to normal when she wakes up.

Chapter Two

Saadiyah was awakened that morning by the vibration of her mobile phone. She stretched her hand to pick up the device from her night stand to see who could be calling her at seven a.m. When she saw her best friend Destiny's name on the screen, she knew that something unusual must have happened. Destiny seldom called her before noon. Saadiyah sat up bracing herself for what she already anticipated to hear.

As-Salamu 'alaykum Destiny, how're you doing?" she uttered with a husky voice, slightly lethargic. Her eyes were half way open as she attempted to adjust to the sunlight coming through the window.

"*Wa 'alaykum Salam* Saadiyah" Destiny responded. "Can you please pick me up? I need a ride."

"Of course I can, where are you? What happened to your car? And why does it sound like you've been crying?"

"Please Saadiyah, just rush and come get me. I'll give you all the details when you get here. I had another argument with Maher, I can't stay here anymore."

"Okay stay strong, I'll be there as quick as possible. Give me just a few minutes to get ready, and I'll be on my way."

As she hurriedly hopped in the shower, Saadiyah felt tears rolling down her eyes. The fights between Destiny and her husband Maher were becoming a regular event now. She felt guilty for not discouraging her friend from marrying that abusive man.

Maher was a friend of Saadiyah's brother Amir. Destiny met him during a sleepover at Saadiyah's parents' house; and she immediately fell head over heels for his looks.

Saadiyah did concede that Maher was a good looking young man, but there was something about his attitude that she had never liked. She felt a drop of arrogance and hostility in his demeanor that made her want to keep away from him. Whenever she mentioned it to Destiny though, the latter just brushed it off as if it wasn't significant. She was in love; that was all that mattered. She refused to look at any flaw that Maher's character might have been predicting about who he was as a human being. Destiny's situation proved once again, that outer beauty when it came to marriage should always come second after the person's inner beauty, their *deen*. Even though Maher did attend the *masjid* regularly, his character wasn't that of a good practicing Muslim.

* * *

Saadiyah and Destiny's friendship went all the way back to middle school, when they were twelve years old in 7th grade. The two became inseparable from the day they met during Math class together. Destiny noticed a boy sitting behind Saadiyah's desk attempting to pull her head scarf. She stood up and commanded him to take his hands off her. She wasn't one to watch bullying go on without intervening. Saadiyah approached her after class to thank her for the act of kindness. She was used to encounters with ignorant bullies due to her dressing differently from the other children, but she wasn't one to let her toes be stepped on either. She stood up for herself whenever she had to. Thank God the majority of people were open minded and respected differences.

Soon, Destiny and Saadiyah started asking their parents to let them sleep over at each other's house. Eventually, even their parents became friends due to the tight bond between the two girls.

***

Destiny was born and raised in the city of West Palm Beach in South Florida. She was the only child, raised by very loving parents. Her father, a wealthy Real Estate Developer who had her when he was in his late thirties, showered her with expensive clothes and gifts; from the latest smartphone to the most sophisticated laptops and tablets. Her mother, who grew up in a middle class family, was the disciplinarian. She often opposed her husband's decisions to spoil the girl that much. She would argue with him that she needed to learn life without having all handed to her. She wanted to teach her daughter to work hard for what she wanted. She feared that if they were to lose their status or worse, die, they would have done disservice to their daughter by making an entitled person who felt like the world owed her everything. She made sure Destiny's gadgets that weren't needs but wants be taken away if she didn't behave in the way she was expected to. She was to keep good grades and a good attitude, both at home and also in school.

Destiny's mother, Jessica, owned a high end shoe and accessories store which she was able to invest in after years of savings while working as an Account Receivable Clerk. She always dreamt about running her own business. Her nonstop efforts paid off in the end.

***

Saadiyah was what is commonly called a first generation American. Her parents moved to the United States of America from Senegal to further their education about three years before she was born. Her father, Munir Job, eventually became a very successful heart surgeon. Her mother Fatima, a skilled accountant, worked for a federal agency in downtown Manhattan.

As time went by, they got accustomed to life in New York City, where their children were eventually born, and loved the little cozy life that they had built for themselves. They feared, however, that New York City would be too challenging for young children. The rough winters were tough enough to endure for an adult, let alone for a child. After a two week trip they had taken down in South Beach, Munir and Fatima fell in love with the laid back lifestyle that the Floridian Peninsula offered. The spacious backyards and large rooms in the Florida homes sealed the deal for them. They were convinced that this was the kind of environment they wanted to raise their children in, close to the beach. The palm trees everywhere around made the residents feel as if they dwelled in a perpetual vacation spot. Soon after that vacation, Munir and Fatima each secured employment in the Miami area. After selling their Brooklyn home, they packed their belongings and headed towards Florida without looking back. With the children only five and three years old, the Job family was ready to find out if the Sunshine State would live up to their expectations. Twenty seven years later, they were still living in Florida.

Chapter Three

"*W*hat's going on this time?" Saadiyah asked her friend when she arrived at her County Line Road home. She found Destiny sitting on the door step, head bowed between her knees. Her red, swollen eyes showed that she had cried all night.

"He threw me out of the house again. Maher slapped me and called me every name in the book under the pretense that I provoked him. He treats me like I am a nobody. He sees it as me being disrespectful when all I did was politely tell him how I feel about what we were discussing."

Saadiyaah clenched her teeth, yet tried to maintain her composure, so as not to make her friend feel worse than she already did. She gave her a tight hug while Destiny burst into tears on her shoulders. She kept on crying for what seemed to be five to ten minutes; then stepped into the car. Saadiyah turned the key in the ignition, grabbed the steering wheel tighter than necessary, and headed towards her house, in East Fort Lauderdale.

As she drove along state Road 441, Destiny gave her more details about the previous night's incident. She recounted that Maher came from the *masjid* after performing the night prayer at nine thirty p.m., and didn't even bother to greet her when he arrived. She knew right away by the angry stare in his eyes that she needed to stay clear of him. She decided to stay in the bedroom to read a *Hadith* book, so as to give him some space and time to cool down. Maher remained in the living room watching television for about an hour before joining her in the bedroom.

Destiny went on to explain that she asked her husband how his day went attempting to lighten the tension in the room. He mumbled a quick response, turned away towards the bathroom and took a very long shower. When he came out, he got dressed, and ordered her to go spend the night in the guest room.

"Why?" I asked him.

"I'm sick of being married to a man. We've been married for seven years now, and you still can't give me any children. Might as well not be married, I'm not getting any younger, I need heirs, children who will keep my legacy going when I'm gone." Maher shouted.

"I told him that he was being unfair to me. It's not my fault that we're still childless seven years after being married. The response that I gave him provided him with an excuse to beat and demean me like he's gotten so accustomed to doing over the past two years."

Maher made it a habit lately to blame Destiny for them not being able to have children. Destiny had been to almost all the gynecologists who practiced in South Florida. They all gave her the same answer after putting her through a battery of tests: There is nothing wrong with you Ma'am; it's just not time for you to get pregnant yet. They advised her to reduce the stress and anxiety levels in her life. They also told her that the more she worried about not getting pregnant, the longer it could take for her to have children. They informed her that the problem might also be coming from her husband. They explained that though it's commonly assumed that infertility is from the woman, it equally affected men. Maher dismissed the suggestion to get examined every time Destiny suggested it. He took it as an attack to his manhood instead of a means to solve their childlessness problem. One of the doctors even suggested that Destiny and her husband take a few months vacation, away from their usual lifestyle and habits, so they could just focus on enjoying each other's company.

When she told Maher about it, he lashed back: "And how do you think our bills will be paid if I stop working for a few months? Do you even use your brain to think sometimes before opening that mouth of yours?"

Destiny had been a house wife for the last four years of her married life. She enjoyed taking care of the home while her husband was at work. She loved preparing his meals, beautifying herself, then eagerly waiting for his arrival from work in order to pamper him, make him feel special each day.

She made the decision to quit her job as a certified nurse when her husband started showing signs of jealousy towards her male coworkers. He would always accuse her of being too friendly with the doctors and other male nurses she worked with.

Being that Maher made enough money to comfortably take care of the both of them, she came to the conclusion that if not working would help her marriage, she would do just that. Her strongest desire was to make her husband happy. She was ready to make the sacrifices required to achieve that.

Saadiyah never understood why her friend would choose to give up a career that was so promising, especially after going to school for many years to obtain the certification she had aimed for since they were teenagers. Destiny had made so many sacrifices, struggling through low paying jobs and sleepless nights in order to pay her way through college. When her hard work was finally being rewarded, she chose to let all of it go down the drain.

Destiny would often recall how Saadiyah was so vocal about the dislike she had for

Maher's manners. But that was before the two of them got married. Once they tied the knot, Saadiyah backed off. Destiny admired her friend's respect for the bond of marriage. She could occasionally perceive looking at Saadiyah, that she was struggling to keep her thoughts about Maher to herself purely for the respect she had for the sanctity of their relationship. She had a strong principle about not meddling into other people's marriages. She would give advice whenever it was solicited, but she made sure never to suggest something that could lead to breaking the marriage vows, no matter how close she was to the person involved. Her stance was to seek solutions to mend instead of break a holy matrimony.

When it came to her marriage though, Destiny wasn't sure anymore if solutions to mend the broken pieces were available; everything she tried so far had failed.

Chapter Four

"*I* want a divorce Saadiyah. He doesn't love me," Destiny asserted, lifting her head high. Determination and sureness were suddenly apparent in her piercing hazel eyes.

Destiny had stopped sobbing, even though her voice trembled with each word.

"Why are you saying that, Destiny? It may be that he just doesn't know how to love. I think the two of you need counseling. He needs to be reminded that our religion teaches us that the best among men is the one who treats his family in the best of manners. Maher needs a reality check. I can't believe that someone who attends prayers and *khutbahs* so often could behave in such a vile manner at home, even get to the point of putting his hands in anger on his wife. This is unacceptable. I nevertheless do have hope that the marriage can still be salvaged. The two of you can't solve your marital problems alone, you need professional help."

Destiny held on tight to the armrest as Saadiyah made a sharp right turn too quickly. She took a deep breath then riposted:

"I'm tired of being the only one in the relationship making concessions, Saadiyah. You're aware of all the sacrifices I've made during the seven years that we've been married to each other. Maher has never really appreciated the efforts that I've made. On the contrary, it seems like the more I work towards the betterment of our marriage, the more he gets angry with me, and rejects me."

Saadiyah did her best to conceal her exasperation. But Destiny could tell by her erratic driving, that she was struggling not to take her straight to the courthouse so she could dissolve any bond that was still tying her to her husband. She pounded on the car horn, glaring at the driver who had just cut them off.

"I know everything that he has put you through, my dear Destiny. It breaks my heart every time you go through hardships at his hands. I deeply wish I could do more than empathize with you. I'll ask my husband to speak with him. It may be that if they spend more time together, Maher may learn from him some basic concepts about how a good Muslim husband should treat his wife."

* * *

Saadiyah not only loved Destiny as her best friend, but she also felt an additional affection towards her that made her want to protect her even more. She was the sister that she did not have. When they were eighteen years of age, freshly out of high school and off to college, Destiny started asking her a lot of questions about her faith. When they were in their early teens, she used to tell Saadiyah often that she wanted to become a Muslim, so she could start wearing a *hijab* just like her. She admired the fact that Saadiyah was less harassed by naughty boys in school than she was. She also loved the beautiful fabrics *hijabs* were made of, the many different ways Saadiyah wrapped them and matched them to her clothing and shoes. Saadiyah would laugh it off, telling her friend that one is not supposed to become a Muslim merely in order to wear a head scarf. The *hijab* had to be the outer display of one's inner faith.

Over the years, Destiny became more serious with her inquiries concerning what Islam was really about. Sensing sincerity in Destiny's queries, Saadiyah started taking her to *Tawheed* classes at the *masjid*. She gave her a Qur'an, along with a *Tafsir* book, so she could understand the Islamic way of life. She took it to heart that Destiny comprehended what becoming a *Muslimah* meant before making the big decision to say the testimony of faith. She had to grasp the understanding behind affirming that there is only One God worthy to be worshipped, and that Muhammad (Peace be upon him) is His servant and Messenger.

About six month after Destiny started learning about Islam there, she became a familiar face at *Masjid As-Saliheen*. She attended Qur'an memorization classes and *Hadith* classes weekly.

She later approached Saadiyah about taking the next step to officially become a *Muslimah*. Saadiyah informed the imam's wife of her friend's wishes. The latter subsequently had her husband come to witness Destiny's testimony of faith, as she started her journey as a *Muslimah*. Destiny was looking forward to facing any challenges that would potentially be lying ahead of her.

Chapter Five

*D*estiny sat on the brown leather sofa while Saadiyah prepared the guest room of her Fort Lauderdale beach home. When Saadiyah was done, Destiny took a long, warm shower, reflecting on what her life had become since she married Maher seven years prior. She had been hiding the extent of Maher's abusive ways from her parents. She now felt guilty about not confiding in her mother. What would be her reaction if she called her without warning to announce that she wanted to get a divorce? What would her father say? How about the extended family? Destiny's tears started rolling down her cheeks again profusely, mixing with the water shooting down from the shower head.

She felt like she had failed her parents, and most importantly she had failed herself. She never lacked anything while growing up. Having been the only child, her parents catered to all her needs without reservation. Even while attending college, she took a job only because she desired independence. They were always there when it came to providing for her or showering her with love. All she could reward them with after their dedication to her success, was to quit her job and become dependent on a man that had no respect for her. Turning off the water, she dried off with a downy scented towel and threw on a pair of pajamas she had borrowed from Saadiyah.

Exhausted from crying so much, and from the lack of sleep, Destiny slipped into the blanket where a subtle lavender fragrance emanated from. It didn't take long for her to fall in a needed restorative sleep. The way she hugged the pillow made her look like a precious little baby under the covers.

***

She opened her eyes a few hours later, wondering what time it was and how long she had been sleeping. She awoke to the smell of a delicious *yassa*. Of all the dishes Saadiyah had picked up from her mother's culture, this was Destiny's favorite.

Destiny got up and walked towards the kitchen where the smell was emanating from. She found her friend standing by the stainless steel stove, greeting her with a cheerful smile that displayed perfectly straight teeth.

"Are you well rested Destiny?" Saadiyah asked. "The *yassa* has been ready for about an hour now, but I kept it warm for you. I know you needed some rest, that's why I didn't wake you. Come and take a seat while I make you a plate."

Destiny finished the first plate of rice within a few minutes; then went for a second helping. She thought about how blessed she was to have a friend like Saadiyah. They understood each other's feelings without needing to say a word. She knew that she could always count on her best friend to be there for her. She was never judgmental about her choices like other women were, especially when they learned that someone was experiencing domestic violence. They would either blame her for staying with her husband, or ask her questions about what she did for him to hit her. They would give her looks that made her uncomfortable, looks that suggested that she must have done him wrong to deserve the beatings. That's why she stopped confiding into anyone other than Saadiyah. She loved her, and knew that it was well reciprocated.

"Is Dawud having lunch at work today?" Destiny asked, sipping on a hot cup of mint tea.

"He already stopped by, and ate while you were asleep. I told him that you were here. He agreed to meet with your husband after work tonight. Hopefully, he'll be able to get through to him."

Destiny admired the relationship between Saadiyah and her husband. It wasn't perfect, but the communication that they had worked on over the years made their marriage a successful one.

Dawud, wouldn't exchange his wife's cooking for any other, unless he didn't have a choice. Even on the days when Saadiyah had to go to work at the bank where she was a well-respected manager, she made sure to prepare her husband a decent meal either the night before, or early in the morning before leaving the house.

It was hard to imagine that such a successful career woman was able to maintain a well balanced life, both as a wife and as a mother of two boys. Saadiyah loved her husband dearly. He was almost entirely what she had dreamt a husband should be. He was so loving, caring, respectful and attentive to his wife's needs.

Dawud never left the house without giving her a loving kiss. He never missed an opportunity to remind her of how much he loved her and appreciated having her in his life. He sent her text messages on a regular basis that said "I love you Saad." or other sweet sayings. That always put a smile on her face and brightened her day.

Every Friday, Dawud came home with a bouquet of beautiful fresh red roses, and a gift bag which contained either an item that he had overheard his wife saying that she wanted, or a caring gift that he thought would make her happy.

He did have flaws. Among other things was the lack of patience that he struggled with. That had the power to sometimes bring Saadiyah close to losing her cool, especially during the first couple of years of their marriage. Over time, she started learning how to forgive his mistake, and vice versa. She also was very hot headed on occasions. What helped them cope with the issues that they encountered within the marriage was that they came to an agreement to discuss anything that came up right away. They refused to leave any room for grudges in their relationship.

The couple strived hard to stay grounded, keeping in mind that no human being on this earth is perfect. Whenever Dawud did something that upset her, Saadiyah would force herself to remember a special thing that he had done for her. Keeping those positive thoughts, even though it was not always easy, made her let go of the mistakes that he made along the way. Dawud on his side, learned over the years to voice his concerns without getting upset like he used to. He constantly struggled to communicate efficiently when he was displeased about a situation. They slowly but steadily adopted the proper attitude to have a successful marriage. They believed that if there is more good than bad in a spouse, then a marriage was worth working on. The efforts had to come from both sides for progress to be made.

* * *

The young couple had met while attending Miami Dade College. Dawud was studying to become a computer engineer; at the same time, Saadiyah was working on obtaining a master's degree in finance. Numbers had always been her passion.

The attraction between them was gradual. They used to see each other at the library almost daily, but neither paid special attention to the other. They were focused on the books that they were studying. Dawud was the first one who eventually noticed Saadiyah. One day he decided to greet her.

"*As-Salamu 'alaykum* sister"

"*Wa 'alaykum Salam;* brother. How're you doing?" Saadiyah replied, surprised to learn that he was a Muslim.

"I'm doing fine, *Alhamduli'Llah*"

From that day forth, they greeted each other whenever they met around the campus. It was during their last year in College that Dawud informed Saadiyah about his interest in taking her as a wife.

Saadiyah felt really flattered by the proposal but managed to keep her composure. She had been observing Dawud for a couple of years. She had never seen him in any compromising situations, unlike so many other young college men. A lot of them used their new found freedom to attend parties where alcohol was served, weed was smoked, and casual romantic relationships were formed then quickly broken. But not Dawud.

She didn't know if she was truly ready to be married. She nevertheless decided instead of giving him a negative response to pray about it; then seek the advice of her parents and Destiny.

Chapter Six

*D*awud woke up around five a.m. on the day that he was to meet Munir, Saadiyah's father, to ask for her hand in marriage. He performed the *Fajr* prayer at the *masjid*. He then went back to his apartment to lie in bed as he usually did, trying to get another hour of rest before going on with his day. He closed his eyes, and tried to empty his mind while relaxing his body. He wasn't able to find the peace of mind that he was looking for this time.

Finally tired of tossing in bed, he decided to get up and go take a shower while listening to a radio podcast. The warm water against his body helped relieve some of the exhaustion he felt. This wasn't the day he needed to appear tired or unkempt. He wanted to make a good first impression in front of Saadiyah's parents. The first meeting could make or break his proposal. She had told him that her father agreed to meet him in the early afternoon.

When he got out of the relaxing shower, Dawud wore a black embroidered *salwar kameez*, which is an elegant long Indian traditional shirt worn over pants made of the same fabric, and headed towards one of his favorite restaurants. He chose to sit by the corner facing a busy street nearby, then ordered chicken Florentine crepes and black coffee. He was surprised to see that he had engulfed the whole plate in one sitting, which he was not in the habit of doing. The stress that he had been feeling seemed to have increased his appetite.

* * *

Munir and Fatima were nothing like Dawud imagined. They greeted him with a very warm welcome, made him feel fully comfortable during his visit in their home. All the fears Dawud had about them being stern and judgmental towards him were quickly dissipated. Munir and he had a long discussion about politics and other subjects of actuality, before shifting to the marriage proposal topic. Munir eventually did ask him the tough questions, trying to decipher through his words the moral values that he lived by. Nevertheless, it didn't feel like an interrogation to Dawud. He knew that this was just a man who loved his daughter, and wanted to make sure that she would be in safe hands with him.

"Have you ever been married?" Munir started.

"No I haven't."

"What type of relationship do you have with your parents and family?"

"My parents are the source of my strength, my role models. They're very hard working. They raised my four siblings and I to be honest, respectful, and most of all, to fear Allah in everything that we do. I'm truly grateful for having been blessed with a tight knit family."

"What makes you think that you can be a good husband?"

"I have three sisters whom I would hate to see mistreated. I have my mind set that I will treat my future wife the same way I would want to have them be taken care of. I grew up seeing my father and mother be partners in all matters, whether it be raising us, handling finances, or any other daily life decisions. I intend to have the same relationship with my wife, hopefully even better."

"How is your relationship with the Qur'an?"

"I have to admit that this past Ramadan was the first time I have read the translation of the meaning from cover to cover. I have memorized the last *juz* over the years while growing up, but I didn't understand most of what I was reciting. *Alhamduli'Llah* I'm now working on getting more knowledge. There are *Tafsir* classes that I just started attending on Friday nights at the *masjid*. The more I learn, the more I discover how much I ignored about my religion. My intention is to make my future children benefit from my experience, and teach them the meaning of what they will learn as they're learning it instead of just focus on memorization."

Munir asked Dawud a few more questions about his expectations in a wife, how he generally dealt with his emotions when it came to anger etc. Dawud answered to all as best he could. There was a moment when he thought that Munir was going to deny his request, but the latter asking to meet his parents gave him the relief he needed to be sure that he had the intention to move forward with giving him his daughter's hand in marriage.

***

The two got married about a month later, after their families had met a few times. Saadiyah never regretted marrying Dawud. He had proven every day since then, that he was the one for her. He knew that it wouldn't always be a smooth road, but he was willing to work with her to strive for path to *Jannah* as man and wife, and leave the rest to Allah.

Three years into their marriage, Jaleel was born, followed by his little brother Jaffar, a couple of years later.

Saadiyah's strongest wish was that her best friend's marriage would be at least as blissful as hers, if not more so. It broke her heart whenever she saw Destiny going through so much hardship at the hands of her husband. She would often reminisce about their innocent discussions from back when they were younger, about how life would be when they would grow up and marry Prince Charming. She considered herself as having lived to see her own dream come true, not exactly as she imagined, but close enough. Now, she was determined to help her friend reach the fulfillment of hers also. There had to be a way to make Maher realize that she was a gem, a precious pearl that he was blessed to have as a wife.

Chapter Seven

$\mathcal{D}$estiny sat in bed for a while, watching Maher sleep. She went from his wide forehead to his distinguished lightly salted and heavily peppered beard, glanced at his high cheekbones and aquiline nose. He looked so peaceful in his sleep. Her heart was filled with love for her husband. She was resolved to do anything within her power to make her marriage work.

The counseling sessions they had been attending weekly, which Dawud reluctantly agreed to, had greatly improved their relationship. Maher took that advice from Amir and Dawud after the last altercation with Destiny. He had promised that he would change, explained that he was just under a lot of stress lately at work which reflected negatively in his family life. One of the employees at the restaurant that he owned and managed had run off with over $15,000 of his profit. He was going through a great deal of hardships trying to fill the gaps, to make sure that his business kept running, in addition to ensuring that the other employees' paychecks stayed current.

Destiny couldn't help but notice how Allah worked in mysterious ways: Every time Maher abused her, he either lost something valuable to him, or he would somehow get into trouble with someone. He even broke his arm once falling down the stairs after throwing water at her when she wanted to pay a visit to her parents. For some reason, he made it a point to alienate her as much as possible from friends and family. Destiny never spoke to anyone about her finding a correlation between Maher's mishaps and the way he treated her, but the guilt she would feel when it would happen made her avoid getting mad at him. The last thing she wanted was for him to be hurt. One thing she was confident about, though, was that Allah was always there for the oppressed. No one commits injustice without it coming back to haunt them.

During their counseling sessions, the imam advised Maher to get accustomed to speaking with his wife about the concerns that he had with his life outside of their home. There was no reason why he should keep his worries from his wife. Our beloved Prophet (Peace be upon him) asked for advice from his wives when faced with difficult situations. He listened to what they had to say and followed their advice.

The imam explained to him that sharing his feelings could lift half of the burden he was carrying, not to mention that she could also give him valuable input which he might not have thought of on his own. The imam went on to make him understand that his wife was his partner, not just someone who was there to have his children. He reminded Maher that when it came to having children, Allah had the final word. They needed to be patient and wait for His time to come. He encouraged him to work on understanding his religion better, because his lack of trust in Allah was evident by the way he dealt with his wife.

Destiny was thrilled about Maher showing signs of comprehension that she was not responsible for them not having been blessed with progeny yet. He started being all smiles whenever he came home from work lately. He returned to being kind and attentive to her needs, just as he used to be when they first got married. He even called her from work every now and then, to find out how she was doing or to ask her not to worry about cooking dinner that day. He instead took her to some of the fanciest restaurants in town. Destiny did her part also. She made sure to keep her husband happy by being a dutiful wife. She vowed in silence that she would make him stay the way he currently was. She was married for better or worse. She wanted to believe that the worst was behind them.

Destiny and Maher's life followed the same routine for a few months. They became great friends and lovers again. She was as fulfilled as a woman could be, except that every month, a negative pregnancy test would find its way to the bottom of the bathroom garbage bin, purposely covered with some tissue paper. She cried every month on the first day of her period. All she wanted was one child... or at least one miscarriage to assure her that she could get pregnant. The wait for another month was always gut-wrenching.

She strived to make every evening special, so that Maher would not tire of intimacy. She didn't neglect anything, from the special care she gave her body, to the sexiest outer wears she could find to spice up the relationship and make herself desirable.

* * *

Destiny sought advice from her mother and from Saadiyah about ways to increase fertility. They both told her there was no special remedy. It was one of those things that none was in control of, except the Almighty. Saadiyah recommended that she increased her *du'as* to Allah. Destiny did just that. She constantly woke up around four a.m. to pray *tahajjud*, begging Allah to grant her at least one offspring. She knew in her heart that Allah answers all *du'as*; it might not be in our own time, but He knew when it was best. She placed her trust in His judgment in all matters.

A few more months went by without a serious argument between Destiny and Maher. One day, she got prepared as she usually did for her husband's return from work. She lovingly concocted a delicious meal, burnt a stick of incense which filled the house with a sweet fragrance. She then ran herself a vanilla scented bath, and lazily laid in it for close to an hour. She went to her closet, hesitated about what to wear for a few minutes before deciding on a long black dress that embraced the curves of her medium built body. Pleased with the way she looked after getting dressed and made up, she sat in the living room to read a book while waiting for her beloved to arrive.

"*As-Salamu 'alaykum*, baby," Destiny greeted Maher cheerfully when she heard the door swing open.

"*Wa 'alaykum Salam*," Maher mumbled with a frown on his face.

"How was your day? You seem to be very tired."

Maher walked fast past her straight towards the room, not even bothering to give her a reply.

Destiny was puzzled. What could be bothering her husband? Everything had been going so great for the last few months. She hadn't seen him in that kind of mood in a very long time. Had she done something wrong unknowingly?

She knew not to push the issue when he was like that.

Destiny plated the salad and shrimp Alfredo that she had prepared for dinner; then cautiously went to the bedroom to ask her husband to join her for dinner. They both ate silently. All one could hear was the noise of the forks and knives hitting the plates. The silence was almost unbearable. When they were done, Maher headed back to the bedroom and turned the television on to a football game.

After she cleared the table up and washed the dishes, Destiny stayed in the living room, trying to delay joining her husband for as long as possible. She had pounded herself with countless questions since Maher came home, but couldn't find any answer to his sudden change of mood. She finally decided that she couldn't run away from the issue indefinitely if there was one. Instead of trying to read his mind, she needed to go and face him. He was her husband, not an enemy that she needed to be afraid of.

Destiny changed into a silk turquoise night gown, slipped under the blanket next to her husband, resting her head upon his left shoulder. Maher suddenly turned sideways and pushed her so hard that she rolled off the bed and landed on the carpeted ground.

Destiny was startled. What had just happened?

"How dare you push me like that Maher? What did I do to deserve this?" she yelled at the top of her lungs as tears of humiliation welled inside her eyes.

Before she knew it, Maher got up, stood above her, and started beating her mercilessly. He continually slapped and kicked her on the stomach while she was still on the ground. Destiny tried to make sense of how things turned to the worst that quickly, but she barely had time to reflect. The pain she felt from the blows was excruciating. Maher's eyes displayed a glow that she saw on some documentaries; a glow that lions' eyes had when they were about to attack their prey. She didn't recognize that man as the one she was married to. The beating for no apparent reason was not happening. It had to be another one of her nightmares. Someone needed to wake her up.

All of a sudden, the room started spinning, everything turned dark. Destiny fell unconscious.

* * *

As Destiny stopped moving, Maher thought that she was bluffing. He kept on giving her blow after blow with his closed fists. Soon, he realized that she had been still for way too long for it to be intentional. He stopped hitting her, and started calling her name, but there was no response to his desperate calls. He sat by his wife on the floor, gently shaking her shoulders in an attempt to wake her. Destiny's body remained limp. He held his head between his hands in disbelief. He knew that he had gone way too far this time. His anger had finally led him to the point of no return. His going to the *masjid* earlier that day where there happened to be an *Aqiqah* going on, had caused him to be beside himself. Destiny didn't do anything to him. He realized how unjust he had become once more. What was he going to do now? What if she was dead? His life seemed to be going on a quick downward spiral as he stared at his wife's flabby body lying on the beige carpet.

Chapter Eight

*D*estiny opened her sore eyes, looked upwards, and saw her mother, Jessica, standing near the bed, wiping her eyes and nose with a white handkerchief. Her father, David, was sitting on a chair nearby, head bent. Saadiyah and Dawud were also in the room. Destiny wondered why Saadiyah was also crying. Her right eye for some reason felt heavier than the left one when she attempted to open them wider. She could barely see through it. Why was everyone at her bedside? She didn't recognize the room. Her lips felt like there were a multitude of cuts on them. She noticed that her arm was hooked-up to some IV tubes. Had she been in a car accident? She couldn't remember any of the events that had led to her being in a hospital room.

She tried, but couldn't word any of the questions that were racing through her mind.

On seeing her daughter open her eyes, Jessica's tears doubled in intensity. She bent her tiny face down and continually kissed Destiny's cheeks. Her dear daughter was alive, that was all that mattered to her at that moment.

Destiny saw Saadiyah rush outside the door. She went to the nurses' station to inform them that her friend woke up.

Dr Grey, a short round faced man, hastily entered the room heading for Destiny's bedside. He thereon, asked the family to give him time alone with his patient. After checking her vital signs and temperature, he pulled a chair near the bed and stated:

"You're very lucky Mrs. Banks. The head trauma that you sustained following the beating you received from your husband could have caused internal bleeding in your brain resulting in much worse damage, even death."

Upon hearing that statement, snippets of the last evening spent with Maher started coming back to Destiny. He had once again betrayed her trust by physically abusing her. She felt warm tears run down her temples, landing inside her ears, then drop onto the hospital bed.

"The bad news is that we couldn't save the baby." Dr Grey continued.

"What do you mean by baby?" Destiny mumbled startled by the statement. She tried to sit up, but a sharp pain pinned her back to the bed.

"Which baby are you talking about, doctor?" she repeated.

"Did you not know that you were roughly nine weeks pregnant?" Dr Grey replied taken aback.

Destiny couldn't believe what she was hearing. The doctor must have confused her with another patient. She tried getting up again, but the pain all over her body pinned her right back down. Did Maher kill their first child? No, it wasn't possible. He couldn't have murdered the baby that they had both dreamt about having for so many years. She would never forgive him if what the doctor said was true.

After Dr Grey spent a few more minutes clarifying the details about Destiny's miscarriage, she was ultimately convinced. He left the room, allowing her family and friends to go back in. Before walking down the hallway, he advised them not to stay too long; she still needed lots of rest.

"He killed my baby, mom," Destiny whispered as she saw her mother's loving face appear through the open door.

Jessica approached the bed and held her daughter's hand. She sobbed even harder. "I know baby, he's currently detained in the Dade county jail. That man doesn't deserve to be your husband anymore; he's a brute."

Chapter Nine

$\mathcal{D}$estiny was picked up from the hospital by Saadiyah about a week after she had been admitted. The swelling in her face had subsided, but the healing scars were still visible on her upper lip and right eye. Her parents wanted her to move in with them, but they both worked full time. Saadiyah insisted that she stay in her home; she had vacation days that she hadn't used yet, so she was going to take some days off and nurse her friend back to emotional and physical health. When Destiny voiced her concern that Dawud was a non-*mahram* to her, Saadiyah reassured her that the couple would make the proper arrangements. Dawud was going to ensure that his wife was there every time before coming home so he and Destiny would never be alone.

Destiny tried not to be bitter, but thinking about her lost pregnancy sparked anger in her at random moments. Tears filled her eyes every time she saw a woman carrying a baby, or upon hearing a baby cry or laugh. The question that kept creeping back into her mind was how she did not feel any signs of pregnancy. She had taken a pregnancy test every month, and they all came out negative. She hadn't missed her menstrual cycle even once. Come to think of it however, her last two menstrual flows were very light; they didn't last as long as the ones she usually had either. It should have given her a clue that she might have been pregnant. Since it was her first time, she didn't recognize those signs.

Then again, continually pondering about what could have changed if she was aware of her pregnancy was not going to help. The past could not be changed; she accepted the *Qadr* of Allah. She firmly believed that Allah had done what was best for her; we may not like some things, but they may be blessings in disguise. She thought about how the situation could have been more complicated if she had a child with Maher. His anger problem might still be triggered by other things. The problem was his character, not their childless marriage.

After spending about two weeks at Saadiyah and Dawud's house, Destiny started applying for jobs in the hospitals and medical facilities located in the Dade and Broward counties. She wanted to get her life back on track; never again would she let herself depend on a man.

Maher had been fined $5,000 to be paid to Destiny for pain and suffering. He was also given a three month jail sentence for domestic violence. She had stopped by what used to be their marital home to pick up her belongings. On her way out, she stood at the door and looked back to see what was left of the feelings of attachment she had for the house and for the one who was her legally married husband. Nothing was left but bitter memories. For her, that was the end of one chapter, and the beginning of the rest of her life.

Looking for a job was a job in itself. Destiny knew that she would be welcome at her best friend's house as long as needed. Nevertheless, as much as she enjoyed having Saadiyah and her children around, she wanted to get an apartment of her own, to move on with her life.

She went from interview to interview. After about three weeks of looking, she was selected for a perfect position at a nearby, highly reputable hospital. Saadiyah advised her not to move out right away; she needed to build some savings for at least a couple of month before living on her own. Destiny took her advice and did not move until she was able to save enough money to buy the things that she immediately needed after moving out. She didn't know what she would do without her friend. Because of Saadiyah, Destiny felt as if she had a blood sister.

* * *

Maher had his head cast down the stairs of the jailhouse. The last few months had been like hell to him. He had never had so many regrets in his life. Destiny had been nothing but a good wife to him. He always found a way to destroy the cozy life that she tried so hard to build for them. He knew that he didn't deserve her love, yet the whole three months that he had spent in jail, he had been thinking about ways to win her love back. He needed her presence in his life; he had to find her and work on making her trust him again. There had to be a way to win back the love of his life.

When he was told in court that she had had a miscarriage, his whole world fell into broken pieces. He wondered if it was going to be a girl or a boy. Would the baby have looked like him, or would he favor his beautiful and well mannered mother? If any, when would they have a chance to conceive again?

No one was on the outside waiting to give him a ride home. The accountant that he hired after his previous one had run off with the money was very honest, and ensured that the business kept running smoothly during Maher's incarceration. He was the only person, besides his lawyer, who visited him weekly while he was in jail. He kept him informed on how the business was doing the whole time that he was away, and kept all the bills paid.

Reflecting upon his life, he didn't turn out too bad financially given the rough childhood he had with an absentee father and a druggy abusive mother. He knew that even though it had been many years, the seed of anger and hatred he constantly felt growing up never left his heart. His failure was that he had let that legacy define his adult relationships, thus potentially destroying his married life.

Maher came to that realization during therapy while he was in jail. He intended to continue seeing a therapist while on the outside. He was determined to end the cycle of violence and destruction that his mother had taught him to perpetuate. It was the only way to stop destroying his life, and the lives of those who loved him. He wanted to learn how to love. For now, he only knew how to hate and display anger.

Chapter Ten

*D*estiny smiled when she saw the name on her mobile phone's caller ID. Saadiyah's voice had the power to brighten her day.

"*As Salamu 'alaykum,* my dear. How is it going?" she answered.

"*Wa 'alaykum Salam.* I'm doing good, *Alhamduli'Llah* sweet pea. How are you?"

"Can't complain either *Alhamduli'Llah.* Hey, I've come to realize that I neglected my well being for so long that I didn't know how being number one in my own life felt like anymore. I've been working on spoiling myself lately, and on taking care of my needs. But first and foremost, I've been rebuilding my relationship with Allah. It seems to me now that I was lacking trust in Allah. That's what caused me to hold on to Maher so strongly instead of letting go when I saw the first signs of bad character. I prayed a lot about getting guidance from Allah for the future of our relationship while I was living with him. He showed me signs that Maher was a violent man, but I never followed my instinct with those clues. I wanted to believe that I could talk him into stopping the verbal abuse, but I was wrong. All that I achieved was allowing him to gradually escalate to physical abuse. I always gave him excuses and blamed myself, especially when he would beg me for forgiveness and promise that it would never happen again. I chose to believe him each time. Now I know that it's never okay to let anyone treat me that way again."

"I'm so happy that you've come to this understanding Destiny. Don't be too hard on yourself though. We judge other people according to our own personality. It's hard for us to imagine that others are capable of doing certain things when we're not inclined to that kind of behavior.

"I feel guilty for advising you to stay and work on your marriage for so long. I would've never forgiven myself if something worse had happened to you. I really hoped that Maher would come to his senses and give you the love that you deserve."

"I know that you meant well, Saadiyah. Please don't feel guilty one bit. I'm an adult who makes my own decisions; I chose to put myself in that situation and also to stay in it. You've always been there for me."

"There was no way you could have guessed that Maher would turn into such a hostile person, Destiny. You didn't choose to get into an abusive relationship. You just happened to be in one because of your trusting nature. You did the best you could to try and make things work. There was nothing that you did wrong. We all make bad choices at times; yours happened to be in choosing the one to marry."

The two friends chatted for some time; then each of them went on with the rest of her day.

***

The following week, Destiny took a day off work to file for divorce. The legal divorce papers would make her free from Maher forever, at last. As she sat down to fill out the paperwork that the clerk had handed to her, she again realized that Allah had done the best for her. She praised Allah that her baby had not survived. It made her feel guilty to have that kind of thought creep into her mind, but she had learned throughout her life that Allah always allows for things to happen for a reason. She thought that even though adversities could be very depressing when one experiences them, down the road, if the person allows herself to be objective, she would find some good in it.

She thought that even her failed marriage had the benefit of showing her how resilient she was. She didn't wish for any woman to ever go through a situation like the one she had lived through, though. She planned on joining an association for women against domestic violence, so other people could benefit from her experience, recognize the early signs of abuse, and leave if need be before things got out of control.

* * *

Maher got served with the divorce papers about a month and a half after he was released from jail. He tried calling Destiny, but her phone number was no longer in service. He attempted several times to get back in touch with her through Dawud and Saadiyah, but they both refused to give him her new address or new phone number. The last time he went to their home, he became so aggressive that Dawud had to ask him to leave.

Not too long ago, Destiny's parents had so much affection towards him, believing that he was a loving husband to their only precious daughter. But now, every time he tried calling them, David and Jessica would hang up on him after using some choice words to show him their disdain.

While reading through the divorce summons, the reality of the last few months hit Maher so hard that he had to sit down, afraid he might pass out. His whole body was trembling. He reminisced about the years that he had been blessed with a beautiful, kind and loving wife. All he did in return was to break her down, belittle her, and worst of all, physically abuse her.

He ached for another chance to be with her. He was determined to prove to her that he would change. He was ready to spend the rest of his life trying to make up for all the wrong that he'd done.

The next day, Maher went to his lawyer's office looking for advice about any legal recourse that could help him avoid a final divorce decree. Subsequent to the lawyer's motion contesting the divorce, the judge ordered mediation between the spouses in an attempt to help them reach an agreement before deciding on a trial date. Destiny reluctantly agreed to that following her lawyer's advice in an attempt to avoid a long trial.

* * *

Destiny entered the imam's office dressed in a long black skirt; her peach colored shoes matched her long sleeve shirt and the flower patterns on her *hijab*. She was more beautiful than ever.

The last person she wanted to see lately was Maher. However, if avoiding a long trial required speaking with him while the imam was present, then she would do so.

Maher was already in the room when she arrived. He got up on seeing her, and walked towards the empty chair near the book shelf to pull it so his wife could sit down. Destiny looked at him, exasperated by the act that just a few month before would have seemed so chivalrous to her. She was tempted to refuse to sit because of the dislike that she was feeling for him, but decided to get past her emotions. She didn't like holding grudges against anyone. She started battling that emotion after she left Maher, because she didn't want to give him or anyone the power to make her feel resentful. That wasn't in her personality; she wasn't about to change.

Destiny respected Imam Sharif, a well grounded man who was gifted with a voice that commanded attention from the listener. He was well known in the community for his integrity and justice. He had carefully read the claims from both the husband and wife before they arrived. After praising Allah as He deserved, he addressed Maher by asking questions about the allegations made by Destiny. To each allegation, Maher agreed that Destiny has spoken the truth;

all of the abuse that she wrote about did take place.

Then Imam Sharif asked Destiny what she wanted from her husband. She replied that all she wanted was her freedom from him. She didn't want any monetary compensation; a divorce was her only request.

The imam then turned his attention back to Maher and said:

"You have taken her as a wife only under Allah's trust; but you broke that trust when you started abusing her. A woman is to be protected by her husband, not broken by him. Instead of making her feel safe in her marital home, you forced her to feel fear and insecurity. You also doubted the *Qadr* of Allah by accusing her of not giving you a child, as if she was the one that decrees what has to happen. I recommend that you give her what she asked for without putting her through any more hardship than you already have. You should also ask her for forgiveness because you have oppressed her, while Allah (Glorified be He) told us that He has forbidden oppression for Himself towards us, and thus has forbidden oppression among ourselves. Anyone who is under your care should be safe from oppression from you. You have failed in your role as a protecting husband."

Destiny looked at Maher as the tears that he tried so hard to hold back rolled down his cheeks, landing on his beard. He pronounced divorce in a shaken voice. Destiny felt a big load lift from her heart. She hoped it meant that she would finally be able to move on with her life, away from Maher and the memories of their broken marriage.

Chapter Eleven

"What a beautiful day for a backyard barbecue," Saadiyah thought to herself as she took the lamb that had been marinating since the night before out of the refrigerator. She sat the red plastic bowl on the counter for some time while Dawud started the fire for the grill outside.

She was hoping that Destiny would give this meeting with Ibrahim a chance. It had been three years since her divorce. Dawud and Saadiyah had tried to arrange meetings with good brothers so many times in hopes that one of them would catch her attention, but Destiny always found a way out of getting to know any of them better. She refused one because she didn't want to deal with anyone who already had children from a previous relationship. She thought another was too talkative; a third one seemed too strict to her and so on. Saadiyah didn't let the rejections deter from her quest. She refused to give up on the idea that her friend would eventually soften up a little, and hopefully find a soul mate.

She had dropped Jaleel and Jaffar off early that morning at her parents' house. Fatima and Munir were always overjoyed to have their grandchildren over for the weekend. Saadiyah knew how much they cherished those moments, so she made sure to take the children to visit them as often as she could. She knew that she would have to give them a reality check after they came back home; nevertheless she wouldn't have had it any differently. She had given up on attempting to convince her parents to be more strict with the boys. They did make sure that Jaleel and Jaffar followed the basic safety rules, but besides that, they allowed them to do anything they wanted to do. They were the ones deciding what food would be included at each meal. They were allowed to stay up until very late each night, no one would get them away from playing their video games or watching their television shows, if that's what they felt like doing. For the boys, going over to Granny and Grand Pappy always felt like the holidays.

Saadiyah asked her husband to open the door when Ibrahim rang the bell a little before eleven thirty a.m. "He is punctual as usual", Dawud had stated to her. Some of the reasons why he had considered him for Destiny were the dependability, conscientiousness, integrity and loyalty that he had the chance to observe in this gentleman's character. Over the years during which they had worked side by side within the same company, Dawud had grown to respect Ibrahim as a coworker and value him for the friend that he had become.

* * *

Destiny arrived when the company was nibbling on baby carrots dipped in ranch dressing. When she first appeared through the sliding glass door, Ibrahim had to struggle against his own soul so as not to stare at her spotless face. She bent her head, shy from being under such scrutiny. Ibrahim kept staring despite his efforts not to, seeming to have been hypnotized by her glowing dark brown skin, her big brown eyes, the refined nose which fit the oblong shape of her face perfectly, and her well-proportioned lips. Dawud had not exaggerated when he mentioned that she was a beautiful woman, Ibrahim observed to himself. He suddenly lowered his gaze, seeming to remember that it wasn't proper to stare at a lady in that manner.

"*As Salamu 'alaykum,*" Destiny uttered, breaking the uncomfortable silence. "Y'all started eating without me?"

Saadiyah smiled while her eyes sparkled, and responded, "*Wa 'alaykum Salam,* my dear. You haven't missed anything. We've been waiting for you. Come and help yourself." She noticed the silent exchange between Destiny and Ibrahim. Her friend's shyness amused her a bit.

Destiny grabbed a disposable plastic plate from the oval wicker dining table and filled it with tacos and guacamole before taking a seat next to Saadiyah, on the opposite side of where Dawud and Ibrahim sat.

She didn't have any desire whatsoever to get to know another man at this point in her life. She nevertheless decided to honor her friend's invitation in order to ease her worries. She had made countless efforts – to no avail – to convince Saadiyah that she enjoyed living her life all by herself for the moment. The past three years had been very beneficial when it came to giving her time to work on knowing herself better, learning to love herself, and pampering herself without feeling selfish. She came to the conclusion that a person needed to have strong self-love before being able to deal with any other relationship.

She enjoyed the delicious lamb kebabs made by the hosts which the company devoured wholeheartedly. They accompanied the meal with a well-prepared garden salad. To crown it all, they finished with a delightful Black Forest cheesecake that Saadiyah made from scratch.

After chitchatting for a couple of hours, Destiny explained that she had to work that night, so she needed to get home. She was looking forward to squeezing in a little nap before work, especially after the delightful brunch she had just indulged in.

Chapter Twelve

Destiny received a phone call from Saadiyah on the Monday following their cookout. She wanted to find out what her impression of Ibrahim was.

Saadiyah also informed her that when Dawud stopped by for lunch earlier, he told her that the man was truly impressed by Destiny's personality. He sincerely desired to know her better, but that could only happen if she also wanted to give him a chance.

Destiny was skeptical; although Ibrahim seemed to be a decent man, she still had strong reservations about going any further with him — or any other man, for that matter. However, she promised to pray *Istikharah* before making any decision, then get back to them with a definitive answer.

Destiny's reply appeased Saadiyah's worries. It was much better than a plain 'no.' All Saadiyah wanted was for Destiny to break the barrier that she had built around herself. She had not allowed any man to go near her since her divorce became final. Once that first layer of ice was broken, who knew what could happen from there?

A few days went by before Destiny finally resolved to make the *Istikharah* prayer. She did think about Ibrahim at times; she acknowledged to herself that he was good looking, as well as fun to be around. The stories that he told kept everyone smiling throughout the few hours that they had spent together. On the other hand, she knew that was not enough to conclude that he could be a good mate. She was determined not to repeat the same mistake she had made a few years back, when she had overlooked Maher's bad qualities due to the infatuation she felt only for the sake of his looks. This time was going to be different. She would take all the time necessary prior to allowing any man into her life, be it Ibrahim or any other.

* * *

Maher paced back and forth in the police department hallway, trying to make sense of the events that led him there. It all started with the phone call that woke him from a deep sleep around one a.m. He was asked to report to the hospital as quickly as possible because his mother had been shot.

The ordeal that took place after that appeared in his brain as one foggy haze. His mother was already in a coma when he barged in to the hospital. An unsettling feeling of unfinished business filled his heart, consumed his mind. He felt cheated out of all the time that he could have spent with her; addiction had stolen it away from him. All he was able to do now was regret and cry incessantly in an attempt to ease the agonizing pain that seized his whole being.

Oddly, he didn't feel anger or spite towards his mother anymore like he used to. Instead, he only felt love, affection, empathy for her. He missed the great mother that she could be whenever she was sober. He longed for the generous, kind woman who ensured that everybody was taken care of before she took care of her own needs. He sobbed deeply for the beautiful woman who had sold her beauty and great personality to the cruel world of drugs and alcohol. Her addiction had cost her happiness, family life, and now her whole life. She went through numerous trips to rehab, but would only stay clean until she met one of her old drug addicted so-called friends. Then, an inevitable relapse followed.

Sergeant Shaughnessy, a tall black man from the Homicide Unit, relayed to Maher that his mother's boyfriend was arrested for the crime. They had a dispute about some drugs that he had purchased, which he suspected was stolen by Anna, Maher's mother. He snapped during the argument, and shot her twice in the head.

Luckily, a neighbor had come out of her apartment to determine the cause of the noise, and she had witnessed the crime. She immediately called the police to report him.

Maher's aunts had arrived at the hospital minutes before Anna was taken off life support. The doctor had already disclosed to Maher the severity of her condition when he had arrived. There was no hope in her ever recovering from so much blood loss. On top of that, the bullets had punctured both her cerebrum and brain stem; she was brain dead. She would never be able to breathe on her own again.

Maher was grateful to have his mother's family around. He was too weak to grieve alone. He had not felt such excruciating pain since the day his divorce with Destiny had been finalized, when he realized that he had wrecked a union that could have been perpetual bliss. He held his mother's hand tightly during the last minutes of her life. It was as if he was feeling her scarred soul depart from her already inert body.

Chapter Thirteen

*I*brahim picked up his glasses from the oak office desk, slipped the temple tips behind his ears, pushed the bridge up a little higher on his Nubian shaped nose, and brought his phone closer to his eyes, to make sure that he was reading the message he just received correctly.

On the screen there were links to web pages. When he clicked on the first one, a page popped up with Destiny's picture displayed on the top left, followed by a long message describing how she was as a person. This was a dating website; the other ones were also websites of the same nature. His cousin Omar sent him this information by email.

Everything had been going so well with Destiny since they had met, eleven months ago. It took him months before being able to gain her trust, but just two weeks prior, she had accepted his marriage proposal... and now this was happening. He felt deeply betrayed by the fact that she could be so double faced. These profiles were created only some days ago, meaning she had already agreed to marry him.

Omar had requested that Ibrahim not mention his name to Destiny about this matter. Questions began to race through his mind. She played him really well, he thought. She seemed like a genuine and honest young lady, yet proved not to be as honest as he had believed. He rushed to Dawud's office to share the news with him, but found it empty. He then remembered that Dawud was traveling to the Keys with Saadiyah that weekend, and was not going to return to the office after *Jumu'ah* prayer that day.

What was he supposed to do now? The one personality trait he could not stand in anyone was dishonesty. He wasn't about to let it slide, fearing that Destiny could end up hiding even bigger matters from him. That wasn't the way he had planned his future family life to be. He would have to be able to trust his partner, or else not get married at all. He grabbed his keys, headed out of the office planning on going home in an attempt to clear his thoughts.

* * *

Destiny was concerned. This was the first time since he had proposed that Ibrahim skipped a day without calling her. Additionally, she tried calling his mobile phone all throughout the weekend and also on Monday morning before heading out to work without getting any response. His phone would ring a few times before going to voicemail. She even left a couple of message. Hopefully nothing bad happened to him or anyone close to him. She was hoping to get some information about Ibrahim from Saadiyah after work, who she also attempted to reach several times to no avail. He figured Destiny did not have service wherever she was. To top it all, Omar was not answering his phone either. Destiny was deeply concerned about Ibrahim's whereabouts. If all failed, she was for sure going to drive to his home after work to find out what was going on.

For now, she needed to focus on giving her undivided attention to the precious babies in the Neo-natal Intensive Care Unit that she cared for.

Although Destiny tried her best to put her emotions aside when caring for her patients, some of them – like baby Jordan, who just came out of surgery due to gastrointestinal problems following a premature birth – did not make it easy for her. Looking at his tiny body in the incubator, hooked up to several tubes, yet making a tight fist held up beside his delicate little face, as if he was showing the world that he was ready to fight against the odds and win the battle to survive, caused tears to well up in the corner of Destiny's eyes.

Whenever she caught herself being emotional, she was quick to regain her composure in order to complete her job duties. She would have time to cry later in the shower. For now, she was going to be strong for these precious infants so she could help save their fragile lives.

She made her first round by checking on the babies' vital signs. This, like her other days in the NICU, would be very busy for sure. The babies needed constant attention and care. However, Destiny wouldn't have it any differently. She felt like it was a privilege to be chosen to help with saving human lives. Nursing was not just a job to her; she considered it a privilege and a test provided by her Creator, an opportunity to positively contribute to society. She was going to make sure to show gratefulness for that blessing by always upholding the best behavior and dedication required by it.

Chapter Fourteen

Saadiyah kept giving quick looks at her watch. She had been sitting in her car waiting for Destiny for thirty minutes. She wondered what was taking her so long to arrive. When she was about to give her another phone call, she saw the burgundy SUV pull up into one of the parking spaces near the mailbox.

"*As Salamu 'alaykum* Dee. What took you so long?"

"*Wa 'alaykum Salam*, Saad. I'm so sorry. We were on code blue; one of our babies went into cardiac arrest about thirty minutes before the end of my shift. I had to stay a little longer than expected."

They entered the gracefully decorated condominium located on the second floor. One could tell from the decor in the living room that the person who designed it had a taste for luxury. From the sofa and arm chairs made of top-grain leather, to the exquisite chandelier hanging on the ceiling, there was no item of the carefully chosen furniture that went unnoticed. It was beautiful and comfortable. Destiny needed to go home to a relaxing environment after the stressful days spent at the hospital. She took it to heart that her time at home would be as restful as she could make it.

She brought two glasses of orange juice, handed one to Saadiyah and went to sit on the lazy boy recliner, lifted the handle to raise her sore feet then turned towards her friend. Saadiyah appeared very nervous, like something was boggling her mind.

"You look preoccupied, Saad. What's going on? I tried calling you several times over the weekend but it went straight to voicemail. I couldn't reach Ibrahim either. Do you know if Dawud heard from him?"

Saadiyah took a sip of the orange juice; then replied: "Are you hiding things from me now Destiny?"

Destiny frowned from the surprising question.

"Why would you think that, Saadiyaah? My life is like an open book to you; there is nothing from it that I would conceal from you."

"Then why didn't you tell me your intentions of joining matrimonial websites? I thought you were serious about Ibrahim."

Destiny was totally confused now. She didn't understand what Saadiyah was talking about. The latter drew her smartphone from her purse, looked up a website and showed it to her.

"What's going on here?" she mumbled while operating the handle on the recliner to lower her feet back down. "Who in the world posted my picture on this website? I don't understand."

Saadiyah looked just as confused.

"You mean that you're not the one who created this profile?"

"Of course I didn't, Saad. I don't even trust meeting people online. You know me better than that."

"That's why I was so surprised." Saadiyah replied. "When Dawud spoke to me about it over the phone, I told him that I didn't believe that you would do something like that. But when he showed me the profile, I saw your picture on those pages, and the description about your personality was so accurate that it started putting doubts in my mind."

"But then if you didn't create these profiles who did? There are at least three links in the email that Ibrahim forwarded to Dawud's inbox."

Destiny was furious that someone was using her information to communicate with other people online. She was going to get to the bottom of that. It explained Ibrahim's sudden disappearance. She felt deeply hurt that, instead of reaching out to her to find out the truth, he chose to keep away, probably judging her in the wrong way.

"We need ask Ibrahim how he found out about these pages, Saadiyah. He's the only one who can give us a lead at this point. Please have Dawud get more information from him. It could be that he's the one playing a game with me. Either way, I need to find out what the truth is."

Saadiyah stayed with Destiny a little over an hour before leaving to go home. It had been a very long day after the lovely weekend she had spent with Dawud in Key West. Thankfully, traffic was lighter at that hour on highway 85 North, between the cities of Hollywood and Fort Lauderdale. She opened the car window to take advantage of the evening breeze. The weather in South Florida was almost always hot year round; one rarely had the luxury of turning the air conditioner off to let fresh air in.

Chapter Fifteen

*E*ven days after the events unfolded,
Destiny was still in disbelief. Would Maher ever
leave her alone?

Maher had been spying on her for years
without her knowledge. She felt betrayed,
violated. She had kept the same password that
she used while married to him, not suspecting
once that Maher – who knew that password –
was still logging in to her email to find out what
she was up to. She never would have thought
that he would stoop that low. He read the
correspondence between her and Ibrahim; then
decided to put an end to their marriage plans in
his own way.

Maher created online accounts under
Destiny's name, sent the links by email, but
inadvertently sent it to Ibrahim's cousin, Omar.
He copied the address from a group email that
Destiny had previously sent to both of them.
Omar recognized her in the pictures, and
informed Ibrahim.

She confronted Maher over the phone, trying to find out why he decided to ruin her personal life after everything that she had endured living with him. Maher could not say anything other than he still loved her and could not stand the idea that someone else was going to marry her.

"I will never be with you again, Maher. You need to understand that. Whether I marry someone else or not, you'll never be part of my life again. I need you to leave me alone, and forever. I allowed you to verbally and physically abuse me for years. No matter how much therapy you went through, I would still resent you if I ever got back with you. I need you to move on with your life, find someone else who will make you happy. Learn from what you did to me, and make sure never to put another woman through the same ordeal. I feel like if I ever got back with you, it would mean that the abuse you put me through was okay… when it wasn't. You always made me believe that it was my fault whenever you hit me. Now I fully understand that it has never been my fault. Although I do forgive you because I know that your spirit was broken from a difficult childhood, I can't forget the years of suffering that I experienced at your hands. I pray to Allah that you find peace and happiness, but it will be without me by your side. Spying on me was low of you. What else are you capable of doing to me? I advise you to keep going to the therapy sessions you said you've been going to; you still have a long way to go before being completely healed. Be grateful that I'm not taking you to court over what you did."

Destiny did not wait to hear Maher's reply. All she heard before hanging up was him saying: "Give us one last chance Dee…" She was done listening to his endless tales.

As a consequence of the test that Maher had put them through, Destiny informed Ibrahim that she was cancelling their wedding plans. Although Ibrahim's attitude could be viewed as legitimate, it had left her with an unsettling feeling. She thought that was a sign not to go any further with the marriage. She had to feel confident that communication would be present between the couple under all circumstances. The fact that Ibrahim chose silence and distance instead of communication left a sour taste in her mouth. At least for now, she was going to remain single. She decided that she would rather be by herself and happy, than with a husband who she was not compatible with.

Chapter Sixteen

*P*assengers waiting to board the cruise ship stood in groups, excitement was palpable everywhere. Destiny handed her parents their boarding passes, then they all headed towards the crowded dock. The burning heat from the sun was toned down by the sea breeze. Destiny was elated about this eight day trip that she was determined to take advantage of with her parents. She looked forward to getting away from South Florida and her routine ever since her parents suggested that she join them on the trip. She definitely had a need to rejuvenate her thoughts, and also to spend more time with her family.

Even though they arrived after one p.m. to avoid the morning rush, the security line was still a little crowded. It took them over half an hour to check in, get their cruise cards, and get through the security line. Destiny didn't mind because she was already on vacation mode in her mind. They reserved spaces on the deck where they planned on taking relaxing sun baths over the next few days. A man from the cruise staff offered to take their luggage, which they gladly handed him. They had packed in their carry-on a few snacks, a change of clothes for each one of them, and a few light items that they thought they would need for the first day. Deciding against going to the crowded buffet, they headed towards the elevator to go to the eleventh floor by the poolside.

Destiny took advantage of the time before the boat left the Fort Lauderdale coast to make a few phone calls. She smiled when she heard Jaleel's voice.

"*As Salamu alaykum,* auntie Destiny."

"*Wa alaykum Salam,* Jaleel. How are you?"

"I'm doing good auntie. Mommy left her phone home when she went to the store."

"Okay dear. How is second grade going for you?"

"Good." The little voice answered.

"Great. Tell mom I called. She may not be able to reach me once we leave because I'm planning on turning my phone off. Let her know that I'll try again as soon as possible."

"Okay auntie."

"Tell your brother that I love you both."

"I will, and I love you too."

Destiny made one last phone call to her bank to inform them that she was travelling. She wanted to avoid having her bank card blocked as they usually did when she would use it in areas that she wasn't used to making purchases. She then turned the device off to devote herself to enjoying her parents' company. She realized that the older she got, the more she appreciated their presence. They were in their mid sixties now; she never wanted to take them for granted, as life was so unpredictable.

* * *

Destiny remembered how David had been so against her reverting to Islam. Thankfully, as time went by, her mother's open mindedness overcame her father's fears. Jessica often brought up the subject by asking Destiny questions about her faith. She was eager to learn about different cultures and faiths, and was open to thoughts that challenged her own beliefs. Destiny used those times to educate them about the Islamic way of life. They discovered that Muslims worshipped the same God that Christians and Jews worship. They were pleased to find out that Muslims believed in Moses and Jesus (Peace be upon them) as prophets and messengers of God. David became aware that his fears were all due to his lack of knowledge of the Islamic way of life and basic belief system. Afterwards, he started bringing up conversations about Islam with his daughter, who was overjoyed and eager to share with her parents the facts of Islam.

* * *

The cruise was as relaxing as Destiny had imagined it would be. Between the lazy days spent on the deck, by the pool and on the suite's balcony, she caught up with the sleep that she had been lacking during the preceding few weeks. She took advantage of the spa as much as she could and enjoyed a couple of massages that she had made sure to reserve from their first day. The Caribbean Islands they visited were each beautiful in their own way. Among other places, they made stops on Key West, the Bahamas, the Grand Cayman, and Jamaica. They took beautiful pictures, and especially, carried memories of a beautiful week spent together as a family.

Upon their return to Fort Lauderdale, Destiny felt some tears well up as she hugged her parents and said good bye. Jessica held her tighter when she saw the glow in her hazel eyes.

"Why don't we have dinner together this weekend?" she whispered.

Destiny nodded in approval and gave her father a quick hug. She rushed towards a cab stationed on the curbside to avoid bursting into tears in front of them.

Chapter Seventeen

*T*he weeks following the cruise went by really fast for Destiny. Routine took over again as soon as she was back, which she actually didn't complain about. Being busy with work was what she wanted, so she often worked double shifts several days a week. On those days, she would fall asleep within minutes of going to bed.

She had seen Saadiyah a few times since she returned from her trip, but it was always short encounters squeezed within their respectively busy schedules. Since each one of them had the afternoon off that Friday, they decided to meet at one of their favorite restaurants for lunch. They loved the hummus and tabbouleh that was served there; the mutton was always tender, juicy and perfectly seasoned by the Lebanese chef as well. On the first bite one could tell that each of their dishes had been prepared by an experienced chef.

Destiny opted for a lamb shawarma with a side salad, while Saadiyah ordered a lamb shank plate which came with rice, hummus, tabbouleh and some veggies. The smell of freshly baked pita bread never failed to bring a smile to Saadiyah's face.

"For some reason, just looking at the food when I come to this place makes me happy... even before I start eating," she stated.

Destiny laughed out loud displaying a row of white oval style teeth and responded.

"I know, you greedy lady. I'd say that tasty food in general makes you happy. I don't know how you still stay in shape even though you indulge in any kind of food you like."

"Ha-ha girl, you know that's a blessing that I inherited from my father's side of the family. When my grandmother was still alive, she was easily mistaken for a teenager if you saw her from the back. I still need to be careful, though, because being skinny does not equal being healthy."

The two friends enjoyed their meal whole heartedly while chatting about various topics. They finally left the restaurant an hour and a half later and headed to the mall, mainly to walk around and digest the meal they had just had. When they exited the mall, a little while later, each of them was carrying bags filled with purchases. They hopped into Destiny's small SUV and headed for her apartment so Saadiyah could pick up her car.

The sun was down by the time they arrived.

"I'll go upstairs with you so I can pray *Maghrib* on time before going home." Saadiyah decided as Destiny pulled into the parking lot.

"Yes, that's better, *Maghrib* goes by so fast that you will miss it if you go straight home."

At the top of the stairs, they were startled to see a tall man standing by Destiny's door dressed in knee length blue jean shorts and a white T-shirt. As they got closer, Destiny recognized her ex-husband and instantly the good mood of the last few hours deserted her. She squeezed her lips tighter together; a frown curved her eyebrows while her heart started beating at a faster pace. Somewhat frightened, she glared at him for a moment, perplexed, not knowing what to think of this unwelcomed visit.

"What are you doing here, Maher?" she eventually became able to verbalize in a rough voice, scrutinizing him in an attempt to read his intentions.

"I'm here to talk to you, Dee. Can we go inside?" he responded in a matter-of-fact tone.

"How can you suggest that, Maher?" Saadiyah reposted to stand up for Destiny. "She is a non-*mahram* to you now; you have no right to come to her residence."

"This is between Destiny and me. Do not get yourself involved in matters that do not concern you, Saadiyah," Maher argued.

"She has told you the truth, Maher." Destiny rebutted with a voice that meant business. "Now please leave as we do not have anything to talk about."

Maher reached out for Destiny's arm attempting to pull the keys out of her hand. In a reflex, Saadiyah stepped in between the two of them. As if that reaction awakened rage within Maher, he pushed her so hard that Saadiyah rolled down the stairs all the way to the landing.

Destiny screamed to the top of her lungs while running down the stairs to check on her friend.

"You've done it again Maher! I hate you and your violence! You haven't changed a bit!" she yelled while warm tears fell profusely down her cheeks. "Saadiyah!" she cried, attempting to pick her up.

She suddenly stopped moving her when she realized that Saadiyah had passed out. She dialed 911 since she knew that the last thing to do when someone falls on their head was to move them.

Chapter Eighteen

*T*he atmosphere in the waiting room was electric. As soon as she arrived at the hospital, Destiny alerted Dawud, then Saadiyah's parents, and finally her own parents. They all were gathered in agonizing pain, waiting for news from the doctors and nurses who were caring for Saadiyah. Amir, Saadiyah's brother, came as soon as he heard the news.

After performing a CT scan then an MRI, one of the doctors informed them that she had severe brain trauma; the diagnosis was diffuse axonal injury due to the fact that her brain had hit her skull back and forth with a lot of force. Saadiyah was still in a coma. The doctors were trying to reduce the swelling of her brain to avoid further damage since surgery was not an option. The doctor explained that she must have been pushed with tremendous force as this type of injury mostly occurs during car accidents.

When Dawud had arrived at the hospital and Destiny gave him the details of what had happened, his first concern after finding out that he couldn't yet see his wife, was to find Maher.

He was ready to strangle him with his bare hands, even if that meant going to prison for life.

"He's already in custody," Destiny explained. "Also right now the last thing you want to do is get yourself in trouble with the law. Your children need you more than ever while their mother gets back on her feet."

Dawud's eyes looked as if they had been injected with blood. Destiny couldn't tell whether it was from sadness, rage, or both.

The doctor who gave them the update a couple of hours back passed by the waiting room door; Dawud run outside to catch up with him.

"How is my wife Doctor?"

"We're still trying to stabilize the swelling. Once we do, we'll move her to the ICU; then you may be able to see her. We'll keep you updated."

"What's going on with her? I need to know, doctor," Dawud cried.

"I'm afraid it's too early to say anything for sure, Mr. Wallace, but I have to be honest with you. Only about ten percent of people with this kind of severe brain trauma do wake up from coma and are able live a somewhat normal life."

Destiny, her parents and Saadiyah's parents all rushed out of the waiting room upon hearing Dawud's guttural scream. Fatima hugged her son-in-law while Munir questioned the doctor about what was going on.

"I apologize but I can only speak with my patient's family about her condition." He said when he saw Destiny and her parents.

"I'm her father." Munir yelled. "Fatima is her mother, Amir her brother, and these other people are close family friends who you have permission to speak in front of."

Dr. Walsh continued:

"There is a ninety percent chance that Saadiyah will remain in what we call a vegetative state for the rest of her life if she gets out of this coma. What I mean is that if that happens, she will be able to breathe on her own; her heart will keep on beating; but her brain will not be able to function anymore. She will not be able to do any of the tasks that we perform in our daily lives."

When the doctor said that, the room erupted with sobs. Destiny's legs refused to hold her weight any longer. She fell on the floor, her back to the wall while endless tears rolled down her aching eyes. She felt grief, but also guilt as she believed that if not for her, Maher would have never harmed Saadiyah. Loathing for the man she once loved grew inside of her until she could taste its bitterness.

In the midst of the cries, a nurse shouted the doctor's name; and he ran back into the room where they were attempting to save Saadiyah's life. Several nurses hurried in and out of the room in turns. None of them had time to speak with the family anymore.

Chapter Nineteen

*D*estiny arrived at the masjid where Saadiyah's *Janazah* would take place around nine in the morning on April the 19th dressed in a black *jelbab* and a dark brown *hijab*. Her face was partially covered with large eyeglasses that she hoped would conceal her red, swollen eyes. Maher had killed two people among those who were the dearest to her. Internal bleeding complicated Saadiyah's fight to stay alive, and in the end, she lost the battle. Destiny had spent the last day and night since her friend's death making *du'as* to Allah, asking Him to grant her forgiveness and Paradise. She promised herself that as long as she lived, her friend would stay in her *du'as*.

Saadiyah's family members were sitting by her in the first rows, a lot of them had travelled in from other states to bid her farewell one last time. From the time that Saadiyah's body was brought into the *musallah* until the *Janazah* prayer was performed, it seemed like no eyes in the room remained dry. Her mother gave a poignant speech to celebrate her life, her accomplishments, her being a dutiful daughter, mother, sister, and friend to the ones who were blessed to have crossed her path. Destiny was too emotional to speak in public. Jessica read the testimony that her daughter had written about her friend on her behalf. Following a couple of more speeches from close relations, those who were Muslim in the assembly stood up behind the imam to perform the *Janazah* prayer.

After the ceremony at the *masjid*, they all proceeded towards the cemetery to lay Saadiyah to her final resting place in this world. When they arrived, Destiny just couldn't handle the idea of seeing Saadiyah's body being covered with dirt. She changed her mind, and remained in her car while everyone else went in to witness the burial.

Destiny requested a few days off from work for bereavement. She desperately needed time to grieve the loss of the one who had been more than a sister to her. Saadiyah understood her without her having to utter one word. She was always there when she needed a shoulder to lean on. They laughed at the same jokes and grieved over the same pains. Whenever she went to bed, it was as if the image of Saadiyah's face would fill the room, her voice would resonate in her ears while she reminisced about their long phone conversations. Destiny felt pain all throughout her body and soul, as if every inch of her was being crushed over and over again. Her endless tears caused her to have a migraine that lasted for days. The only thing that appeased her was to pray, which she did almost constantly.

Within two weeks of Saadiyah's passing, Destiny started packing her things. She wasn't able to walk up or down the stairs anymore without being haunted by the vision of her friend's body laying there. She preferred paying the penalty to break the lease than to keep on reliving that agonizing nightmare. She strongly considered moving out of state. However, due to the fact that she was the only witness to Maher's crime, she would then have to come back to Florida for the investigation and upcoming trial. She already dreaded the day when she would have to face that monster again. Deciding it was best to be not too far from her parents, she chose to move to Fort Myers for the time being.

Chapter Twenty

$\mathcal{D}$estiny walked through the toy aisle looking for the best thing to buy for Jaleel and Jaffar. After examining what was available, she concluded that a toy was not the best choice. They already had too many of those. She opted to buy books for them instead. It had been two years since their mother had passed away, and they had grown so much since then. Saadiyah would have been so proud of them. Jaffar was in third grade now and Jaleel in fifth grade. Destiny visited them every weekend when they went to their grandparents' home. Seeing them made her very emotional at times thinking about how their mother had been deprived from watching them grow into such fine little men.

Time had passed by so quickly, yet so slowly. She missed being able to pick up her phone and dial Saadiyah's number, hear her voice and have a long conversation with her about all kind of topics. She wished that she would still be able to tell her about her day after work, make her laugh at some silly jokes… Alas, she knew that Allah is The Most Wise, and His will must always come to pass. No one is on this earth forever.

One thing that made life a bit easier for Saadiyah's family and for Destiny was that Maher had pleaded guilty. He accepted a plea deal that the family consented to because they wanted to avoid the strain of a lengthy and painful trial. Because he was a repeat offender, Maher risked being sentenced to life in prison without the possibility of parole if he was found guilty in a jury trial. Considering that, he agreed to a sentence of thirty-five years, with possibility of parole after twenty-five. Destiny was grateful that she never had to see him again. What amazed her, though, was that she still found herself making *du'a* for him occasionally. Despite the fact that she couldn't stand him, she prayed that Allah would guide him, and inspire him to repent before he died. She somehow felt pity for his soul.

With books in hand, Destiny rang the doorbell to Fatima and Munir's home, only to be tackled by the children, all cheerful to see her. Their running towards her jumping and hugging her firmly with their tiny arms had the power to relieve her body of all stress. The children returned the unconditional love that she had for them tenfold. Seeing them smile was truly priceless.

* * *

When Destiny announced that she was ready to take her leave after spending the afternoon with the children and Saadiyah's parents, Fatima asked to first have a moment alone with her. Destiny knew that this was bound to happen again, she wasn't going to be able to avoid addressing the request that her late friend's mother had been talking to her about for several months now.

She walked with Fatima to the home office where she now did most of her accounting work. Fatima pulled a chair for Destiny; then took a seat facing her.

"So, Destiny, what answer do you have for me?" she asked with a big smile on her face. "You promised that you'd give me a definite one today."

Destiny grinned. The embarrassment she felt was obvious as she put her head down, staring at the blue carpet.

"I don't know, Mom. It just doesn't feel right." She had gotten used to calling Fatima 'Mom' over the years. She deeply loved her as if she were family.

"There's nothing wrong with marrying Dawud, Destiny. Moreover, I'm positive that Saadiyah would totally approve of a union between the two of you. She always wanted for you what she wanted for herself. Munir spoke to Dawud about it and he agreed a long time ago. There's nothing to feel guilty about as Saadiyah is not among us anymore. Her children love you. I personally would trust you over anyone to be my grandchildren's step mother. I know in my heart that Saadiyah would feel the same way."

Tears suddenly welled in Destiny's eyes.

"I know, Mom. I've prayed *Istikhrah* about it several times since the first time you mentioned it to me. I have a good feeling about it. Yet, I feel like that would be a betrayal of the close friendship I had with Saadiyah."

"You can't make *haram* what Allah has made *halal*, Destiny. If this kind of marriage was immoral, then Allah would have made it *haram*," Fatima argued.

"You're right. I guess if I look at it that way it will ease the guilt that I feel about it."

Fatima stood up and hugged Destiny for a while. They both cried tears mixed of sadness and relief.

* * *

The wedding ceremony between Destiny and Dawud took place at Destiny's place with a few of their family members, Saadiyah's family members, the imam who officiated, and a few other people who were accompanying him. Destiny had chosen it that way because she didn't want a big wedding. After the imam recited the verses that befitted the occasion, he gave a sermon advising the bride and groom about the life that they were about to begin as husband and wife. He then asked them in turn if they accepted to conclude the marriage contract.

Both Dawud and Destiny agreed. Their faces were both beaming with joy.

Allah worked in mysterious ways, Destiny thought. Never for a second during Saadiyah's lifetime would she have thought about being with Dawud. But now there she was, united to him in holy matrimony. She prayed in silence to Allah for Him to always keep their love pure, their marriage successful, filled with everlasting love; for Him to keep their children protected, and bless her friend's soul with rest in Paradise.

Arabic terms

Alhamduli'Llah: All Praise is due to Allah - God

Allah: The name Muslims call God

Aqiqah: a celebration of the birth of a child by sacrificing a sheep or goat and distributing part of this meat to the poor.

As-Salamu 'alaykum: Peace be unto you

Deen: Religion

Du'a: Supplication made to Allah

Fajr: Time for the dawn prayer

Hadith: compilation of events and teachings from the life of Prophet Muhammad (Peace be upon him)

Halal: Permissible

Haram: Forbidden

Hijab: head scarf

Imam: person who leads the prayers in a masjid

Istikharah: prayer to seek Allah's guidance in a matter before making a decision

Janazah: Funeral prayer

Jannah: Paradise

Jelbab: Long dress

Jumu'ah prayer: a prayer offered in congregation at the masjid every Friday afternoon

Juz: The Qur'an is divided in thirty parts, each of them is called a juz in Arabic

Khutbahs: religious sermon

Maghrib: time for the sunset prayer

Mahram: someone you're not allowed to marry, like your father, mother, brothers, sisters, direct uncles, direct aunts, grandparents, children and step children.

Masjid As-Saliheen: Name of the masjid, meaning Masjid of the Pious

Masjid: Mosque. The house of worship for Muslims

Musallah: the prayer area within the masjid

Muslimah: Female Muslim

Qadr: Predestination

Qur'an: The Muslims' Holy book

Tafsir: a book that explains the verses of the Qur'an, when they were revealed, what each verse applied to, and how the Prophet Muhammad – Peace be upon him – interpreted them to his companions and followers

Tahajjud: Voluntary prayer made in the middle of the night

Tawheed: Indivisible Oneness concept of Monotheism in Islam, Indivisible Oneness of Allah

Wa 'alaykum Salam: And upon you be peace

Yassa: A dish from Senegal made of chicken and onions seasoned with lemon juice, with a side of white rice

About the author

Amina N. is a Muslim woman who lives in Roswell Georgia. Although she resided most of her life away from her birth country, Senegal, she kept within her all the great values from her culture which she was taught while growing in the welcoming city of Dakar.

She always loved reading and writing, loves taking care of animals and watch them interact with each other. Being a very spiritual person, she enjoys spending time alone and long moments of silence; she yet would not trade spending time with her daughter, friends and family for anything.